The Brothers Grimm
The Elves and the Shoemaker
and other fairy tales

Miles
KeLLY

First published in 2015 by Miles Kelly Publishing Ltd
Harding's Barn, Bardfield End Green, Thaxted, Essex, CM6 3PX, UK

2 4 6 8 10 9 7 5 3 1

Publishing Director Belinda Gallagher
Creative Director Jo Cowan
Editorial Director Rosie Neave
Designer Rob Hale
Production Manager Elizabeth Collins
Reprographics Stephan Davis, Jennifer Cozens, Thom Allaway

ISBN 978-1-78209-744-0

Printed in China

British Library Cataloguing-in-Publication Data
A catalogue record for this book is available from the British Library

ACKNOWLEDGEMENTS
The publishers would like to thank the following artists who have contributed to this book:

Front cover and all border illustrations: Louise Ellis (The Bright Agency)

Inside illustrations:
The Elves and the Shoemaker Ayesha Lopez (Advocate-art)
Rumpelstiltskin Kristina Swarner (The Bright Agency)
The Golden Goose Polona Kosec (Advocate-art)
The Star Money Martina Peluso (Advocate-art)

Made with paper from a sustainable forest

www.mileskelly.net
info@mileskelly.net

Contents

The Elves and the Shoemaker

Once upon a time, there lived a shoemaker who became very poor. At last he only had enough leather left to make one more pair of shoes. That evening, he sat sadly at his workbench, drew the shapes for

the shoes, and cut them out. "I'll sew these together in the morning," he sighed. "Once they're made and sold, heaven knows what will happen to me." And he shuffled off to bed.

Next morning, the shoemaker went back to his workbench, and was amazed to see the two shoes quite finished on his table. He blinked, and rubbed his eyes, and pinched himself – but he wasn't dreaming, they were still there. The shoemaker was totally flabbergasted.

He reached out nervously and picked up the shoes. Very carefully, he turned them over in his hands. They were so neatly made that he could hardly see the stitches! They were the most beautiful pair of shoes that he had ever seen! The shoemaker sighed and scratched his head. Then he put the shoes in his window and opened up the shop, feeling totally bewildered.

He didn't have long to wait before a customer came in, eager to buy the shoes. The woman paid the shoemaker a very good price. The shoemaker couldn't believe his luck. Now he had the money to buy enough leather for two more pairs of shoes!

That night, he sat at his workbench

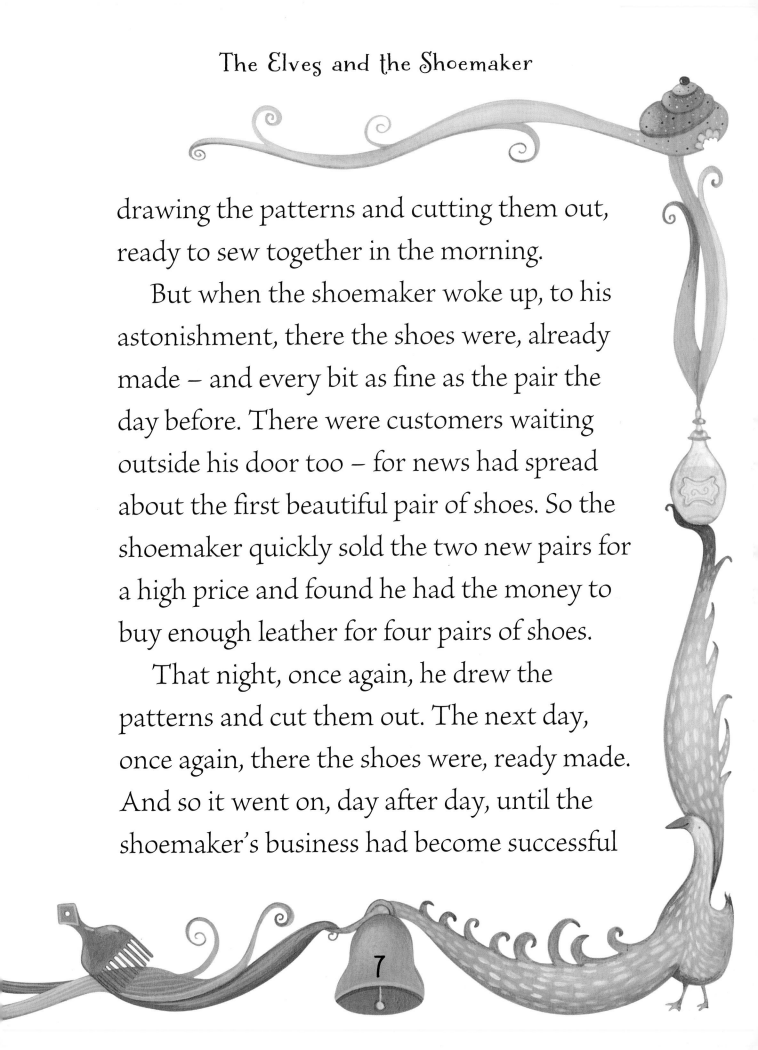

drawing the patterns and cutting them out, ready to sew together in the morning.

But when the shoemaker woke up, to his astonishment, there the shoes were, already made – and every bit as fine as the pair the day before. There were customers waiting outside his door too – for news had spread about the first beautiful pair of shoes. So the shoemaker quickly sold the two new pairs for a high price and found he had the money to buy enough leather for four pairs of shoes.

That night, once again, he drew the patterns and cut them out. The next day, once again, there the shoes were, ready made. And so it went on, day after day, until the shoemaker's business had become successful once again and he had become a rich man.

One evening, the shoemaker said to his wife, "Why don't we stay up tonight and see if we can spot who comes and helps us?"

The shoemaker's wife thought it was a great idea. They left a candle burning in the workshop and hid behind a curtain.

They peeped out and waited, and at midnight two teeny-tiny men crept into the workshop. They were smaller than the shoemaker's little finger and wore simple, raggedy clothes and caps. They sat down at the shoemaker's workbench, picked up all the leather which was laid out, and began to stitch, and sew, and hammer. They were so skilful and quick that the shoemaker and his

wife couldn't take their eyes off them. The little men didn't stop until all the leather was stitched into beautiful shoes. Then away they ran into the night.

The next morning the shoemaker's wife said, "Those little men have made us rich, and we really must thank them for it. Did you notice how tatty their clothes were? I'll tell you what we should do: I'll sew them new little shirts, and coats, and vests, and trousers, and you make them two tiny pairs of shoes."

So that is what they did.

A few nights later, when everything was ready, they laid their presents out on the workbench and hid behind the curtain.

At midnight, the teeny-tiny men came

creeping in as usual – and how happy they were to find their new outfits! They hurried to put them on at once, then they danced about with glee.

Then the two little men skipped away into the night… and the shoemaker and his wife never saw them again. But they didn't need them anyway, because from then on, they always seemed to have good luck in all that they did.

Rumpelstiltskin

Once upon a time, there lived a miller and his daughter. They were very poor and the people round about looked down on them. So one day the miller told a terrible fib about his daughter, to make them

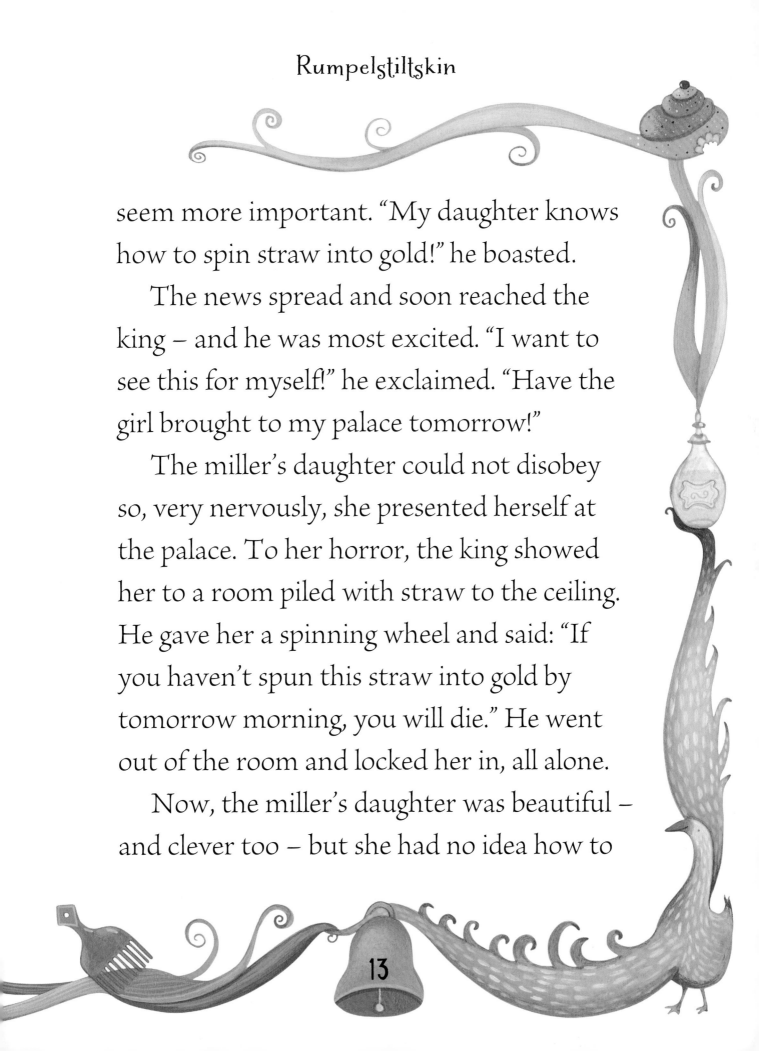

seem more important. "My daughter knows how to spin straw into gold!" he boasted.

The news spread and soon reached the king – and he was most excited. "I want to see this for myself!" he exclaimed. "Have the girl brought to my palace tomorrow!"

The miller's daughter could not disobey so, very nervously, she presented herself at the palace. To her horror, the king showed her to a room piled with straw to the ceiling. He gave her a spinning wheel and said: "If you haven't spun this straw into gold by tomorrow morning, you will die." He went out of the room and locked her in, all alone.

Now, the miller's daughter was beautiful – and clever too – but she had no idea how to spin straw into gold. She began to weep.

All at once the door creaked open and in came a strange little man. "Good morning, Miss," he said. "What are you crying about?"

"I have to spin straw into gold – and I don't have a clue how to do it," the miller's daughter sobbed.

"What will you give me if I do it for you?" asked the little man.

The miller's daughter thought fast. "My bracelet!" she cried.

The little man took the bracelet. Then he sat at the spinning wheel and – *whirr, whirr, whirr!* – he span all day and late into the night. Finally all the straw was gone – and reels of pure gold covered the floor! Then the

little man strode out and the door locked itself behind him.

At daybreak the king arrived. When he saw the gold he was astonished and delighted! But he was greedy. He took the miller's daughter to another room. It was even larger – and it too was piled with straw to the ceiling. "Now let's see you do it again," the king said. "If you can't, you will die." And he went out and locked the door.

Once again, the girl sank down and began to cry, when the door opened and there was the strange little man.

"What will you give me if I help you again?" he asked.

"The ring on my finger," the girl offered.

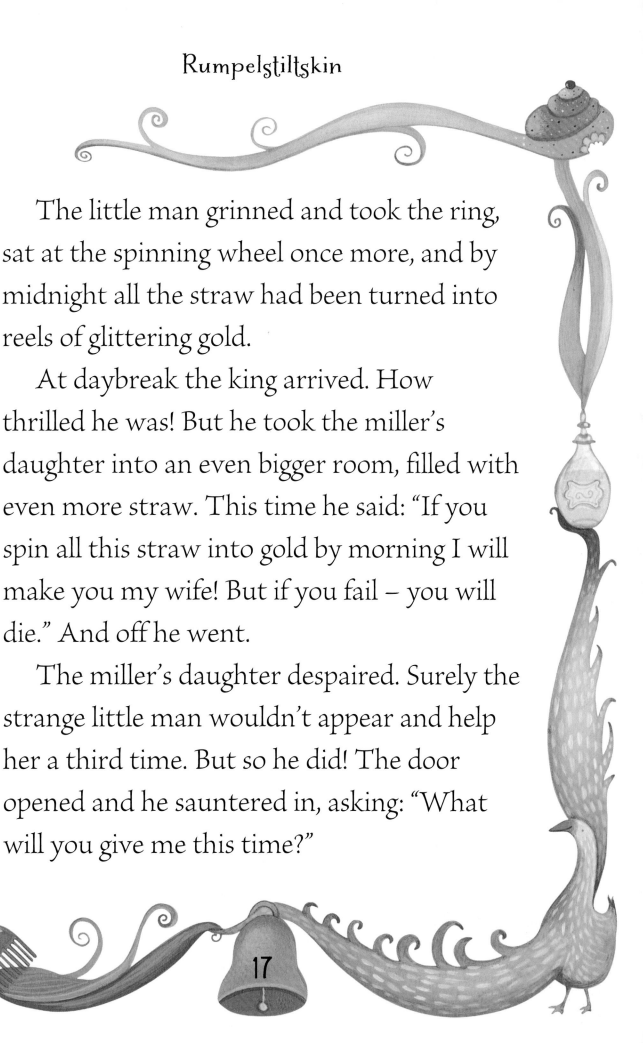

The little man grinned and took the ring, sat at the spinning wheel once more, and by midnight all the straw had been turned into reels of glittering gold.

At daybreak the king arrived. How thrilled he was! But he took the miller's daughter into an even bigger room, filled with even more straw. This time he said: "If you spin all this straw into gold by morning I will make you my wife! But if you fail – you will die." And off he went.

The miller's daughter despaired. Surely the strange little man wouldn't appear and help her a third time. But so he did! The door opened and he sauntered in, asking: "What will you give me this time?"

The miller's daughter hung her head. "I have nothing left," she said, hopelessly.

Then the little man's eyes glinted. "Promise me," he said, "that when you become queen, you will give me your first-born child."

The miller's daughter had no choice. If she did not promise what the little man wanted, she would die. With a heavy heart, she said: "I promise," and the little man sat down and span all the straw into gold.

Next morning, when the king arrived, he could not believe his eyes. He kissed the miller's daughter, and the following day he married her.

The queen found her new life with the

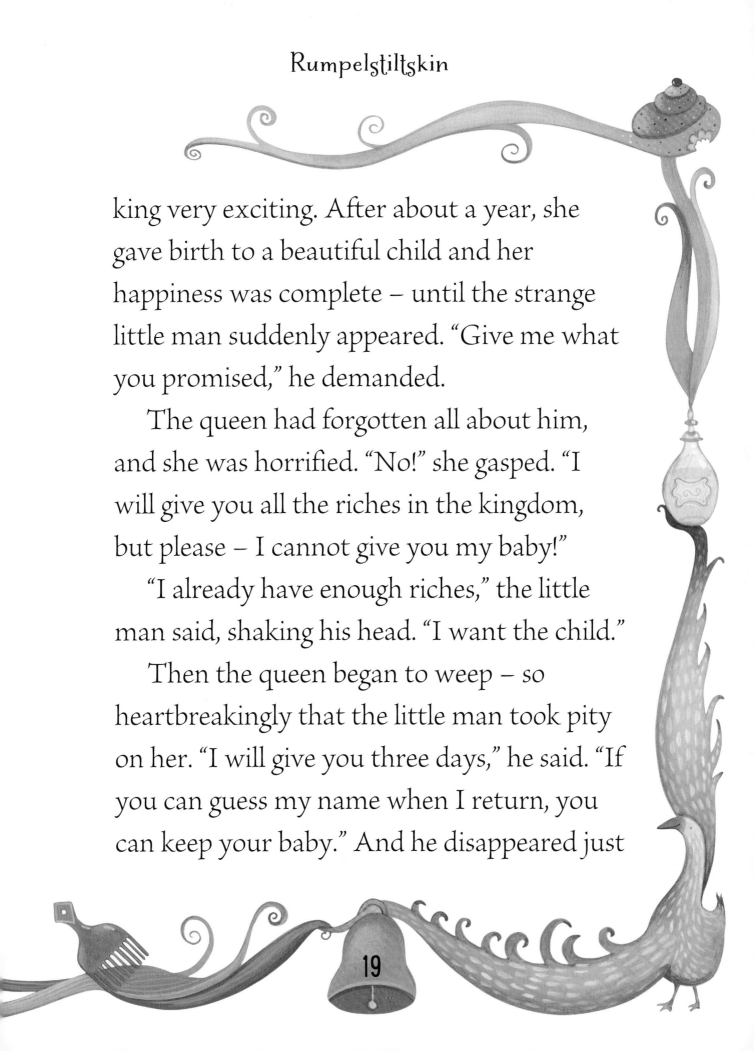

king very exciting. After about a year, she gave birth to a beautiful child and her happiness was complete – until the strange little man suddenly appeared. "Give me what you promised," he demanded.

The queen had forgotten all about him, and she was horrified. "No!" she gasped. "I will give you all the riches in the kingdom, but please – I cannot give you my baby!"

"I already have enough riches," the little man said, shaking his head. "I want the child."

Then the queen began to weep – so heartbreakingly that the little man took pity on her. "I will give you three days," he said. "If you can guess my name when I return, you can keep your baby." And he disappeared just as suddenly as he had arrived.

All night, the queen thought frantically of every name she had ever heard. The next day, when the little man appeared, she ran through her whole list: "Is it Caspar?… Melchior?… Balthazar?…" and so on.

But the little man just answered: "That is not my name," to each one. And when the queen had read out every name, he giggled and disappeared.

Straight away, the queen sent out messengers to search for other names. So the next day, when the little man appeared again, she had another list. "Perhaps your name is Shortribs?" she asked. "Or Sheepshanks?… Or Laceleg?…" and so on.

But the little man just answered: "That is not my name," to each one. When the queen had run out, he laughed and vanished. The queen wept.

Late that evening a messenger returned to the palace and told her: "I travelled until I came to a mountain where there was a little house. A little campfire was burning outside, and round the fire danced the most peculiar little man I have ever seen.

He was singing a strange song. The words were: 'I'll win the game! For no one can guess that Rumpelstiltskin is my name!'"

The queen was overjoyed with the messenger's news. When the strange little man appeared on the third morning, she was quite calm and ready.

"Is your name…" she pretended to wonder. "Might it possibly be… Is there any chance at all that you could be called… *Rumpelstiltskin?*"

"SOMEONE TOLD YOU!" roared the little man, hopping up and down, totally enraged. "WHO TOLD YOU?"

But the queen refused to tell, and in his anger Rumpelstiltskin jumped up and down

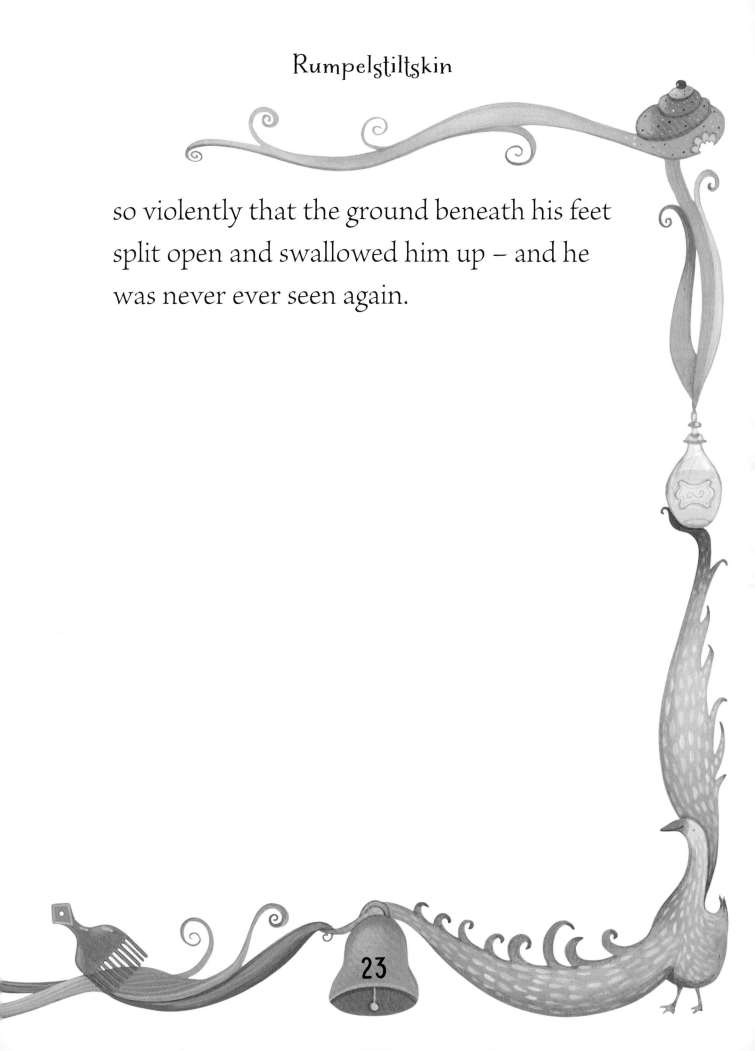

so violently that the ground beneath his feet split open and swallowed him up – and he was never ever seen again.

The Golden Goose

Once upon a time there was a man who had three sons. The youngest son was called Duffer. Everyone thought he was a fool and laughed at him.

One day, the eldest son went into the

forest to chop wood. His mother packed a cake and some juice for him, so he wouldn't be hungry or thirsty. As he was hacking away at a tree, a little grey-haired old man came up to him. "Can I have a bite of your food and a drop of your drink?" he asked. "I am so hungry and thirsty."

"I've only got enough for myself," the young man answered. "Be off with you!"

The little grey-haired man strode away through the trees. The young man picked up his axe and swung it again at the tree – but he slipped and missed the tree entirely, cutting his leg instead. He had to limp home in horrible pain.

The next day, the second son went into

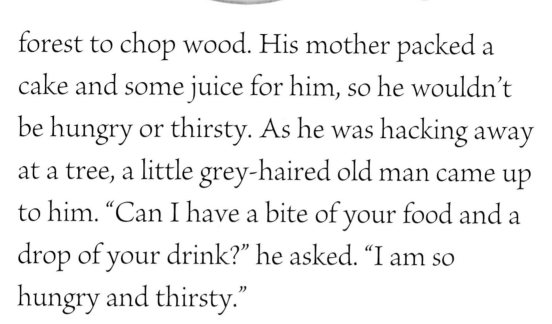

the forest to chop wood. Again, his mother packed a cake and some juice for him. The little grey-haired man came up once more and, like his brother, the young man refused to share his lunch. The little grey-haired man strode away and, with the very next axe blow, the young man struck himself in the side. He had to hobble home in agony.

On the third day, Duffer went into the forest to chop wood. His mother sent him off with only some dry biscuits and water. He was hacking away at a tree when the little grey-haired man came up and asked him for food and drink. "I don't have anything very much," said Duffer, "but I will happily share it with you."

So they sat down, and when Duffer pulled out his biscuits, they had turned into cake, and his water had become juice. So the two ate and drank quite happily together.

When they had both eaten enough the little man said: "Since you have a good heart, I will give you good luck. Chop down that old tree over there and you will find something precious at the roots." Then the little grey-haired man

strode off, whistling cheerfully to himself.

Duffer did as he had been told and chopped down the old tree. To his great surprise, there was a goose sitting in the roots. But it was no ordinary bird, for its feathers were made of pure gold! He picked her up carefully and went off to an inn where he thought he would stay the night.

Now the innkeeper had three daughters, who couldn't believe their eyes when they saw the golden goose under Duffer's arm. They all wanted a closer look.

That night, the eldest waited till everyone was sleeping, then crept into Duffer's room. She tiptoed over to the golden goose and stroked the wing, thinking she might pull out

a golden feather for herself. But her hand stuck fast! No matter how much she pulled, she couldn't let go!

Not long afterwards, the second girl came creeping in. She too wanted a golden feather, and reached out to stroke the golden goose. But before her sister could say 'Don't touch it!' she too was stuck fast!

Then the third girl came, and the others hissed: "Keep away, for goodness' sake!" But she wasn't listening, she was so dazzled by the golden goose. She reached out to take a feather – and there she was, stuck fast too!

All three sisters had to spend the night with the goose.

In the morning Duffer woke up, picked up

the bird and strolled out with it, not the slightest bit worried about the three girls hanging on to it. They were forced to run after him wherever he went!

In the middle of the fields, they met a vicar who said: "Young ladies, it's not proper behaviour to run after a young man like that – stop it at once!" He grabbed the youngest girl's hand to pull her away. But as soon as he touched her, he was stuck fast too!

Duffer walked on, with the three girls and the vicar trailing behind him. Before long a farmer came by. He was amazed at the sight and said, "Good morning, vicar, where are you all going?" The farmer touched the vicar's sleeve – and he was stuck fast too!

Duffer walked on, with the three girls, the vicar and the farmer trotting along behind him. After a while, they came across two farmworkers labouring in the fields. "Hey, you lads!" called the farmer. "Come and help me!" But as soon as the farmworkers touched him, they were stuck fast too!

Now there were seven people running behind Duffer and the goose: the three girls, the vicar, the farmer and the two farmhands.

Soon they came to a city. In this city lived a king who had a daughter who was so serious that no one could make her laugh. The king had announced that whoever could cheer up his daughter and make her giggle could marry her.

Of course, the minute the princess saw Duffer and his golden goose walking past her window, with the girls and the vicar and the farmer and the farmhands stuck fast behind them, she chuckled and chortled and burst out laughing until tears ran from her eyes.

The king couldn't believe

his ears. He was delighted that his daughter had laughed at last. But he didn't want her to marry Duffer! He decided that he must find a reason to put off the wedding.

The king told Duffer: "I will let you marry the princess, but first you have to find a man who can drink a cellarful of wine."

Duffer thought straight away of the little grey-haired man who had helped him before. He went into the forest and fetched him, and the little man drank the king's cellar dry!

Then the king told Duffer: "Of course I will let you marry the princess, but first you have to find a man who can eat a huge hill of bread."

So Duffer asked the little grey-haired man to help him once more, and the tiny fellow ate a massive mountain of bread!

Then the king told Duffer: "I will definitely let you marry the princess, but first you have to find a ship that can sail on land as well as on water."

Duffer asked the little grey-haired man, who snapped his fingers – and a ship that could sail on land and on water appeared.

Then the king saw that Duffer was far from a fool after all – there was no way he was going to get the better of him! The royal wedding went ahead, with much celebrating and rejoicing. The couple lived happily together; Duffer made sure that the princess

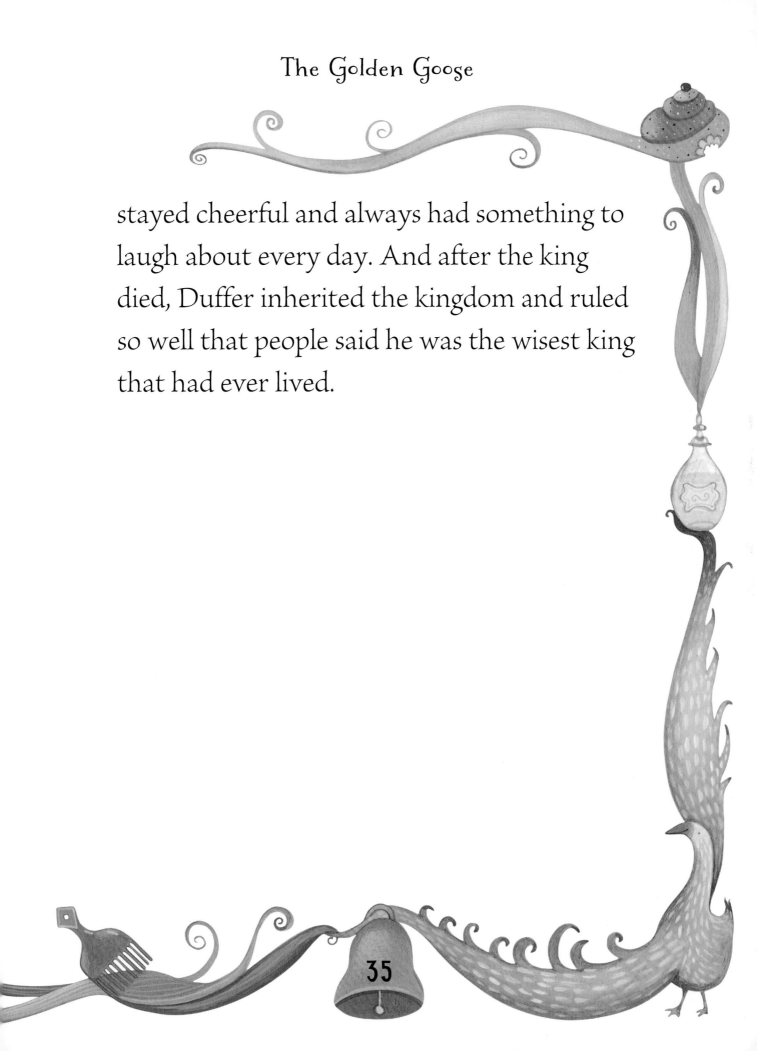

stayed cheerful and always had something to laugh about every day. And after the king died, Duffer inherited the kingdom and ruled so well that people said he was the wisest king that had ever lived.

The Star Money

Once upon a time, there was a little girl whose father and mother had died. She became so poor that she could no longer afford to live in their tiny house. She had to go out into the world with only the clothes

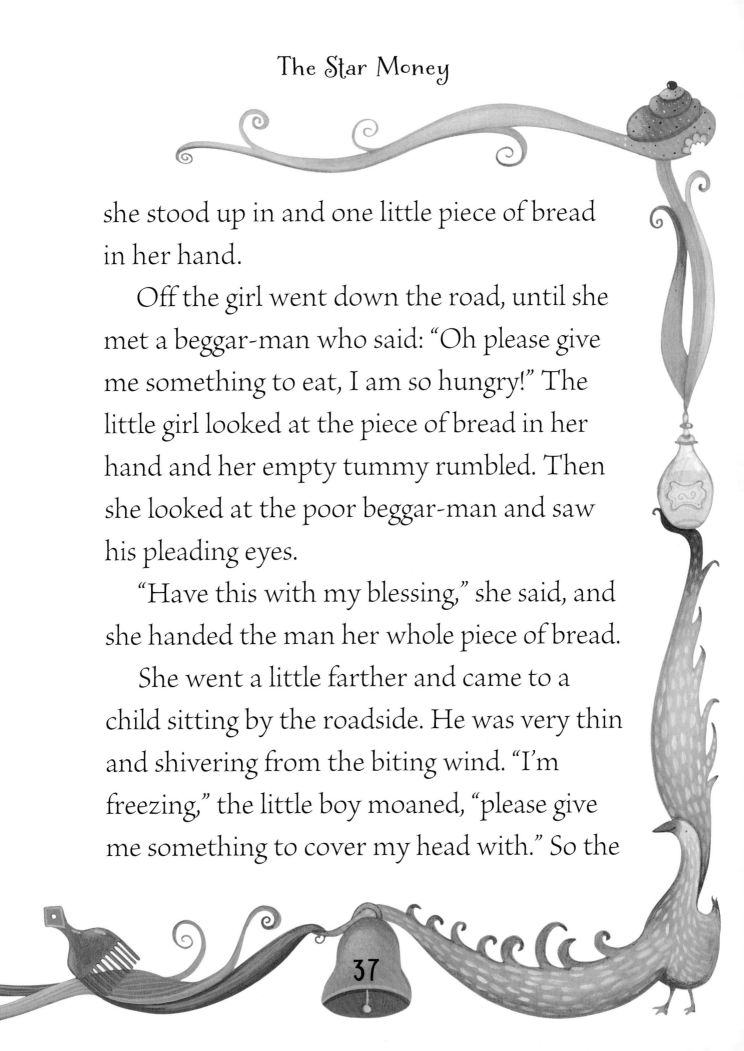

she stood up in and one little piece of bread in her hand.

Off the girl went down the road, until she met a beggar-man who said: "Oh please give me something to eat, I am so hungry!" The little girl looked at the piece of bread in her hand and her empty tummy rumbled. Then she looked at the poor beggar-man and saw his pleading eyes.

"Have this with my blessing," she said, and she handed the man her whole piece of bread.

She went a little farther and came to a child sitting by the roadside. He was very thin and shivering from the biting wind. "I'm freezing," the little boy moaned, "please give me something to cover my head with." So the little girl took off her hood and gave it to him.

Down the road she went, until she came to another child, even poorer and colder than the first. He stared up at her with dark, sunken eyes in his ghostly pale face.

The little girl took off her jacket and wrapped it around the boy's shoulders, with a gentle smile.

A short way further on, the little girl saw a bundle of rags in a doorway. She drew closer and, to her horror, saw that it wasn't a bundle of rags,

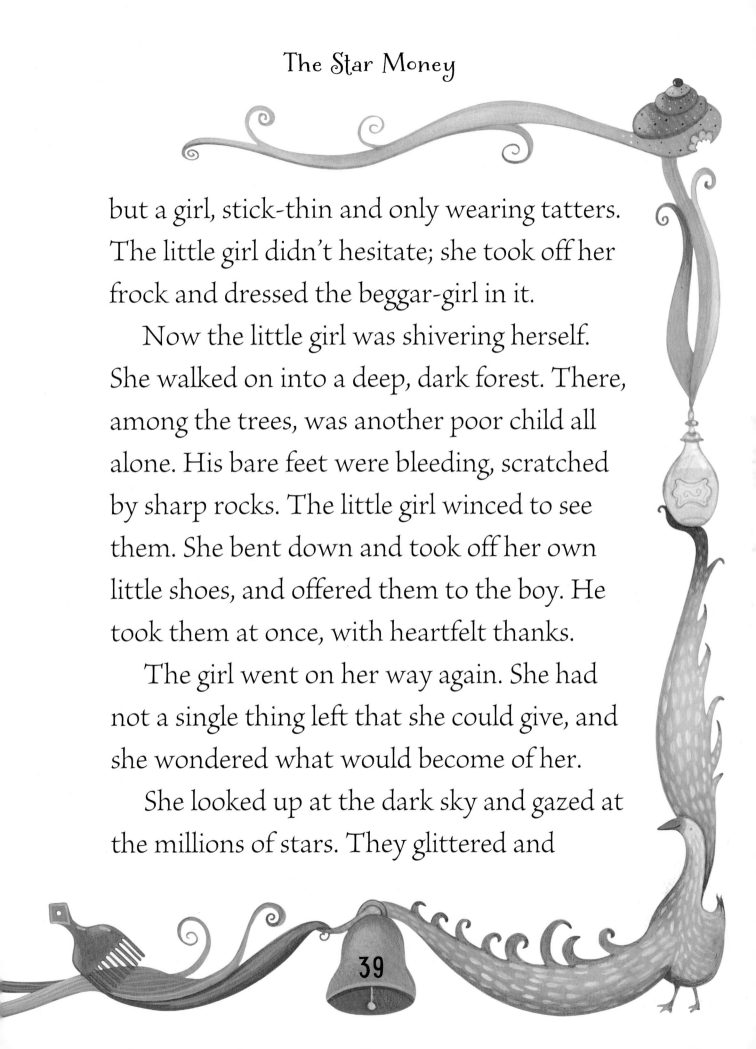

but a girl, stick-thin and only wearing tatters. The little girl didn't hesitate; she took off her frock and dressed the beggar-girl in it.

Now the little girl was shivering herself. She walked on into a deep, dark forest. There, among the trees, was another poor child all alone. His bare feet were bleeding, scratched by sharp rocks. The little girl winced to see them. She bent down and took off her own little shoes, and offered them to the boy. He took them at once, with heartfelt thanks.

The girl went on her way again. She had not a single thing left that she could give, and she wondered what would become of her.

She looked up at the dark sky and gazed at the millions of stars. They glittered and twinkled... and began to fall from the sky. The little girl thought she must be dreaming – but shining coins were falling all around her. She clapped her hands and hurried to gather as many as she could carry.

Then she was rich all the days of her life – and lived happily ever after.